Molly's Magic

The Invisible Bunny

Look out for the rest of the series

Another title from Hodder Children's Books:

SEA LEGS

Alex Shearer

"How do you mean − 'just go anyway', Clive?" I asked.

"I mean we could just sneak onboard," Clive said, "sort of find ourselves an empty cabin somewhere and just sort of settle down for the trip. I mean, let's face it, it has to be better than looking at that big corduroy patch on the bottom of Grandad's trousers ..."

Twins Eric and Clive can't see how their plan to sneak onboard a luxury cruise liner − just to be near their dad, the Head Steward − can possibly fail! OK, so Clive is a compulsive liar, with a tendency towards disastrous mishaps, but it's worth the risk. All they have to do is stay out of Dad's way and stay out of trouble − for three whole weeks.

Easy ...

Another title from Hodder Children's Books:

HOW TO TRAIN YOUR DRAGON

by Hiccup Horrendous Haddock III
translated from the Old Norse by Cressida Cowell

ABOUT THE AUTHOR

Hiccup Horrendous Haddock III was a truly extraordinary Viking Hero. Warrior chieftain, awesome sword-fighter and amateur naturalist, he was known throughout Vikingdom as 'the Dragon Whisperer', on account of his power over these terrifying beasts.

But it wasn't always like that ...

'A classic.' *The Viking Herald*

'*How to Train Your Dragon* is a must-read for every Hero who is having a little trouble being as Heroic as he would like to be.' *The Barbarian Librarian*

Molly's Magic

The Invisible Bunny

HOLLY WEBB

Illustrated by Erica Jane Waters

SCHOLASTIC

First published in the UK in 2009 by Scholastic Children's Books
An imprint of Scholastic Ltd
Euston House, 24 Eversholt Street
London, NW1 1DB, UK
Registered office: Westfield Road, Southam, Warwickshire, CV47 0RA
SCHOLASTIC and associated logos are trademarks and/or
registered trademarks of Scholastic Inc.

Text copyright © Holly Webb, 2009
Illustration copyright © Erica Jane Waters, 2009

The rights of Holly Webb and Erica Jane Waters
to be identified as the author and illustrator of this work
have been asserted by them.

Cover illustration © Erica Jane Waters 2009

ISBN 978 1 407 10752 3

Printed by CPI Bookmarque, Croydon,CR0 4TD
Papers used by Scholastic Children's Books are made from wood grown in
sustainable forests.

1 3 5 7 9 10 8 6 4 2

Th | WILTSHIRE | | :ion
incidents | | |
or are used f | | | or dead,

| JF | PETERS |
| 12-Feb-2009 | |

For Alice, with love

Chapter One

The Birthday Party

Molly pulled on her favourite pink jeans, and her T-shirt with the puppies on it. She'd bought it with her pocket money the last time Mum had taken her shopping. The puppies looked so like her friends Star and Stella, the wish puppies, that she hadn't been able to resist it.

Molly smiled at the puppies. She hadn't seen Star and Stella for a while, and she hoped they weren't wearing out their new owner too much. Mrs Hunter was quite old. Molly had helped to bring Star and Stella back together after Mrs Hunter had bought Star, without knowing that she was a magical wish puppy and needed her twin. Molly had been the only person who could tell what was really wrong with Star when she had come into Molly's dad's surgery. Sometimes being able to talk to magical animals was a big help!

Molly grinned at herself in the mirror.

By the time Kitty's birthday party was finished, she was bound to be covered in cake and ice cream, but at least she could start off looking nice!

Kitty was downstairs already, in her new purple birthday dress, with no less than six *I am 4!* badges on. Mum had tried to persuade her not to wear them all, but Kitty was being stubborn, and it *was* her birthday, so she'd got away with it.

"Is he here yet? Is he here yet? When *will* he be here?" Kitty was jumping up and down by the living room window, which looked out on to the lane. "Can you see him, Molly?"

Molly looked out. "No. Who?"

"The Amazing Albert! The magician!" Kitty stared at her as though she were mad. Then she went back to the window.

"Oh! Look at that car! That has to be his car!"

A beautiful old red Rolls Royce was purring slowly up the lane, and turning into the yard outside Larkfield Vets, Molly and Kitty's home. Kitty raced back to the kitchen door and out into the yard, watching as the Rolls parked outside their dad's surgery. An elderly man got out, wearing a red tailcoat, with the most enormous white moustache Molly had ever seen. He spotted Molly and Kitty at once, and bowed, very low. Kitty was delighted, and curtseyed back, holding out her purple dress.

Molly's dad came out to help the magician carry in all his boxes, and Kitty's guests started to arrive too. Molly was kept busy showing them where to put their presents, and telling everyone where

to go, but she couldn't help peeking out into the back garden every so often. She hadn't been very excited when Mum said there would be a magician, but that was before she saw the Amazing Albert. He just looked – well, magical.

It was a wonderful afternoon, really

sunny, even though it was the beginning of October. The magic show was set up in the garden, with all the children sitting round on shiny red cushions that the magician had brought with him. Dad had joked that he must have a magic car, he'd fitted so much stuff into it, but the Amazing Albert had just smiled.

The magician was now wearing a tall, scarlet top hat as well. He looked brilliant, and all Kitty's friends gasped when he made bunches of flowers appear out of nowhere (he gave them to Molly's mum). Then he juggled with flaming torches, and rode on a unicycle. At last, he blew the torches out, and crouched down closer to the children.

"Do you like my hat?" he asked, in a very serious voice, and everyone nodded.

He swept it off his head, and held it

out in front of him. "Would you like to see what's inside it?"

"A bunny rabbit!" Kitty gasped excitedly, and the magician laughed.

"Not yet. Look, completely empty. But now..." He put in his hand, and felt around, frowning. "Where's she got to?" Then he poked his nose into the hat, and everyone giggled. "Snowdrop! Where are you? Aha!" And he pulled out a beautiful snow-white rabbit, her fur sparkling in the sunshine. "This is Snowdrop!"

The rabbit stared round at the children, her nose twitching with interest. She was the prettiest rabbit Molly had ever seen, with big dark eyes, and almost silvery-looking fur.

"Now, Kitty, as it's your birthday, Snowdrop and I would like you to help us with this next bit. And perhaps your big sister too," the Amazing Albert added, looking thoughtfully at Molly. "That's it, come on out here. Now, I shall put Snowdrop back..." He laid a red silk handkerchief over the top of the hat, and then whisked it away. "And you can see, everyone, the hat is now empty! Now, Kitty and Molly, see if you can lift her out again."

As soon as Molly reached into the hat with Kitty, and touched Snowdrop's silky fur, she knew that she wasn't just any rabbit. There was a wonderful warm, tingling feeling rushing through her fingers, and the hat seemed to be full of pink sparkles — her fingers were glittering.

And when they pulled Snowdrop out of the hat, she wasn't a white rabbit any more.

She was pink!

Molly gasped, and everyone in the audience *oooh*ed with delight. Snowdrop looked up at Molly, and Molly was *almost* certain she winked. Then she went back to staring innocently out at the audience.

Molly could hardly sit still for the rest of the magic show, she was so excited. Snowdrop simply had to be magical.

Not everyone was as convinced as Molly was, though. Her cousin Louis was sitting at the back next to her, and he just looked bored. He was a couple of years older than Molly, but they got on pretty well.

"Isn't she brilliant?" Molly whispered excitedly.

Louis looked at her disgustedly. "Oh, come on, Molly. You don't believe it's real magic, do you? It's all a trick. It's obvious!

You can't really make a rabbit change colour!"

Molly just stared straight ahead, smiling a little. Maybe not. But a *magic* rabbit could do it all by herself...

At the end of the show, Albert invited everyone to come and stroke Snowdrop. Molly was desperate to go up, but she hung back, hoping that all the others would want to go and start tea, and she might get a moment to talk to Snowdrop without anyone listening.

They were the only ones left in the garden now. Shyly, Molly went up to the Amazing Albert's table, where Snowdrop was sitting while the magician packed away his tricks. Was it her imagination, or was Snowdrop staring at her too?

"Please may I stroke her?" Molly

asked politely, and the magician smiled.
"Of course!" He twirled his moustache,
watching Molly thoughtfully.

Molly put out her hand to stroke
Snowdrop's ears, but the white rabbit
shook her head, and jumped straight into
Molly's arms instead. Molly gasped – she
could really feel Snowdrop's magic now.
A wonderful warmth was running all
the way down to her toes, like she was

drinking sparkly hot chocolate.

"You *are* magic!" Molly whispered happily. "I thought so!"

"Well, you are too!" the rabbit promptly replied. "Didn't I tell you?" she demanded, looking over Molly's shoulder at the magician.

"Yes, yes, I know, she can hear you talking." He was nodding delightedly. "Snowdrop said she thought you were different, when you pulled her out of the hat. And of course, when she came out pink, I knew there was something special about you. Snowdrop doesn't turn pink for many people."

"Can you do other colours too?" Molly asked Snowdrop, impressed.

Snowdrop looked smug. "Of course. Any colour you like!" she boasted. "Even stripes!"

"Only on a good day," Albert reminded her. "At that party last week you were a very plain brown, *and* you smelled of fish."

Snowdrop sniffed, and twitched her ears as though she didn't like to be reminded. "He was a very unpleasant little boy," she said loftily. "He was picking his nose. Molly is *nice*. Look!" Snowdrop wrinkled her nose, and closed her eyes, and then her tail turned purple.

"Oh, that's fantastic!" Molly giggled.

"So Molly, tell me, have you always been able to talk to animals? Snowdrop's never spoken to anyone but me before, this is a most exciting day for us!" Albert twirled his moustache with one finger, making it curlier than ever. He looked really delighted to have met Molly.

Molly beamed at him. "No, I only

realized a few weeks ago. I met a magic
kitten called Sparkle, and then two wish
puppies, Star and Stella. But that's all. I've
never met a magic rabbit. And I only
know one other person who can talk to
animals – Sparkle's owner. She's a witch
who lives in Larkfield Wood."

Albert nodded. "It's a rare gift, and very
special. Oh my goodness!" He checked his

watch. "Snowdrop, we must go! We have another party, Molly. I'm sorry we can't stay, but I'm sure we'll see you again."

Molly helped him carry his boxes to the car and waved them off, then she wandered slowly back to the party, smiling happily to herself.

She'd met a witch's kitten, and two wish puppies, and now a magic rabbit. A rabbit who could change colour, and vanish into a hat. Albert was right — it was a wonderful day!

Chapter Two

The Hiccupping Bunny

Molly wasn't sure how she was going to see Snowdrop and Albert again. She wished they hadn't had to dash off so quickly. Albert had said they would meet again, but Molly couldn't see how. It was all a bit disappointing – she'd met a gorgeous magic bunny, and she'd hardly had a chance to talk to her! She couldn't stop thinking about rabbits all week, and her teacher told her off for drawing rabbits on her science worksheet.

On Friday afternoon, Molly ran over to the surgery to see if her dad wanted any help. She looked interestedly round the waiting room, and wondered why the man in the brown jacket looked so familiar. He was bending over a box on his lap, but when he looked up, Molly recognized the moustache at once – it was Albert!

"Molly!" He sounded very pleased to see her.

Snowdrop popped her head out of the box at once, her whiskers twitching with delight. "Hello!" she whispered, as Molly crouched down next to her.

"Snowdrop?" Molly's dad was looking round the surgery door. "Oh! Aren't you...?"

"The Amazing Albert, yes." Albert smiled.

"Kitty's still talking about you!" Dad waved them in. "So, what's wrong with Snowdrop? She seemed very healthy at the party. Beautiful condition."

Albert lifted Snowdrop out and cuddled her. "It sounds silly, but – she keeps getting the hiccups. It started a few days ago, soon after Kitty's party, actually. They go on for so long, and I'm just a bit worried about her. She's never had them before."

Molly's dad looked intrigued. "Well, I've never had that one before." He looked at Snowdrop thoughtfully. "No other symptoms, just hiccups? I might have to go and look that up... Would you mind waiting a minute?"

As soon as Molly's dad had gone, Albert gave Molly a worried look. "I couldn't really tell your father, Molly, but it's *not* just hiccups..." He stroked Snowdrop anxiously. "She disappears! Not always, but every so often, she hiccups, and then she vanishes! I don't know what to do!"

Molly looked at Snowdrop, expecting her to be worried too, but Snowdrop almost looked as though she was smiling. "It's fun," she whispered to Molly.

"Yesterday we did another birthday party, and Snowdrop started hiccupping inside my top hat. I could feel it shaking! And then when she was supposed to disappear, she did, but she didn't come back!" Albert shook his head worriedly. "I had to pretend it was part of the show."

Snowdrop wriggled crossly in his arms. "I did come back, in that special present," she reminded him. "Everyone was very impressed!"

"Yes, but it was in the pass-the-parcel," Albert explained to Molly. "And they were impressed, but that little girl's mother was very confused, Snowdrop. She couldn't work out where the box of crayons had gone. Nor can I, for that matter."

Molly could just imagine what her

mum would have said if she'd found a
rabbit in Kitty's pass-the-parcel. "And
you really don't have any idea why?" she
wondered, watching as Snowdrop wriggled
out of Albert's arms, and went to explore
the rest of the surgery.

"No," Albert sighed. Then he murmured,
very quietly, so Snowdrop couldn't hear,
"And I can't help worrying, what if next
time she doesn't come back?"

Just then Molly's dad came back in, still
holding a very large book on rabbits and

everything that could possibly go wrong with them.

"I *think* she may just have an upset stomach," he said. "Not too serious. I'll give her some soothing medicine, and you need to keep a careful eye on her diet. No lettuce!"

Albert looked relieved, but then he frowned. "Is there any chance it could be catching?" he asked worriedly.

"Well, it could be a virus, yes. Like stomach flu in humans," Dad agreed.

Albert shook his head. "Oh well. I suppose I'll have to cancel," he said sadly.

"What's wrong?" Molly asked. "Do you have another party?"

"No," Albert sighed. "A big magicians' conference, in Edinburgh. I'd been quite looking forward to it, but it starts tomorrow and I won't be back until

Tuesday. I can't risk Snowdrop giving hiccups to all those other rabbits, it just wouldn't be fair."

Snowdrop was scrabbling at his trouser leg, and he picked her up and stroked her ears sadly. She gazed round at them all, her eyes anxious.

"Snowdrop could stay here at the vet's!" Molly suggested excitedly. "We'd look after her for you, then you'd still be able to go."

"Oh, Molly, hang on," Dad said, shaking his head. "Normally I'd say yes, of course we could, but we're really busy this weekend, and Jenny's on holiday, remember? Jenny's our veterinary nurse, Albert. I'm really sorry, I'm just not sure we can fit in looking after Snowdrop too."

"I'll look after her!" Molly said eagerly.

She was standing on tiptoe, gazing hopefully up at her dad and Albert.

"I could, honestly. I know loads about rabbits, I really do."

"I'm not sure, Molly..." Dad murmured doubtfully.

"I could! Dad, I'm nearly eight, you know! Lots of my friends have pets. I'm not too young, I promise."

"It *is* only for a few days," Albert put

in, looking at Molly's dad pleadingly. "I'm sure Molly would look after Snowdrop beautifully. They seemed to get on very well at the party."

"And if Snowdrop's tummy upset got worse, Dad, she'd be in the right place!" Molly pointed out.

Snowdrop wrinkled her nose, and gazed at Molly's dad too.

Molly was almost sure she heard a faint tinkling sound, like little bells, and the air seemed to shimmer pink for a second. She caught her breath. Was Snowdrop doing magic?

Dad shook his head slightly, as though he was feeling dizzy. Then he looked thoughtfully at Molly. "Oh, all right..." he sighed. "But you're going to have to be very responsible, Molly."

Then Snowdrop winked at her. There

was no doubt about it this time. Snowdrop
had magicked her dad into saying yes!

"Wonderful!" Albert cried, hugging
Snowdrop. "I'll bring Snowdrop's hutch
round tomorrow morning before I leave."

"We could put it in the shed, couldn't
we, Dad?" Molly suggested. She really
wanted her dad to see how much

she knew about looking after animals.
"Rabbits shouldn't be outside all night
now it's getting chillier. And we get foxes
around here. She'd be much safer in the
shed. I can go and tidy it up, Dad! You'll
get a tidy shed too!"

"Mmm." Dad still didn't sound
convinced, but at least he wasn't saying no.

"Thanks, Dad," Molly said, putting an
arm round him. "Honestly, I'll look after
Snowdrop so well. You'll see!" Molly
just couldn't keep the smile off her face.
She went to stroke Snowdrop's nose, and
whispered, "You're coming to stay with
me!" It was so exciting!

Snowdrop gave her whiskers a delicate
little shiver, and they glittered pink for a
second. She looked excited too.

Molly sighed happily. At last she was
going to have the chance to show Mum

and Dad how well she could look after
a pet. It was almost as if her special wish
puppy wish for a pet of her own was
starting to come true!

Chapter Three

Snowdrop Settles In

Molly got up super-early on Saturday
morning to tidy the shed ready for
Snowdrop's hutch. It wasn't much of a
fun job. The shed was full of gardening
tools, and seed packets, and spiders. Kitty
kept trying to help, and then shrieking
and running away whenever she saw
even a leg of a spider. But it was worth
it to have a pet, even if Snowdrop was
borrowed, and only Molly's for three days.

Snowdrop's hutch was huge. It almost

filled the back seat of Albert's car, and Dad had to help him carry it in. They set it up in the shed, and then Albert took Snowdrop out to say goodbye.

"Be good!" he told her firmly. "Don't be naughty for Molly. And *please* try not to hiccup!" he added in a whisper. Then he handed her to Molly, and looked worriedly at them both. "I do hope you'll be all right," he murmured. "I've never left her with anyone else before."

"You'll be late if you don't set off soon," Snowdrop told him. "Molly and I will be fine. Won't we?" There were pink sparkles fizzing round her ears, and she had a look of mischief in her eyes.

Molly nodded happily. "We really will!" she promised. She hadn't noticed Snowdrop's mischievous glance.

Albert handed her an enormous bag

of carrots. "Her favourite..." he muttered. Then he rushed off to his car, without looking back.

Snowdrop was Molly's now!

It was wonderful, having a pet, especially one who could talk back! Molly spent most of the day in the garden with Snowdrop, chatting, although of course they had to be careful when Mum or Dad or Kitty were around. Snowdrop was very funny. Molly soon discovered that she liked to have things her own way, and she was quite fussy. She liked eating daisies, but only the yellow middles, and she insisted that Molly had to pick the petals off one by one, as they tasted better that way. Molly tried pulling all the petals off at once when she wasn't looking, but Snowdrop spat that one out, and gave her a reproachful look.

"Sorry..." Molly said, trying not to laugh. Snowdrop's face was so funny. After that, she didn't try to argue when Snowdrop demanded that her stomach medicine had to be fed to her drop by drop on wafer-thin slices of peeled carrot. It was easier just to do as she was told.

"Molly! Teatime!"

Molly jumped up. "Oh, that's Mum. I'll

pop you back in your hutch, but don't
worry, I'll come back out to see you after
tea."

Snowdrop nodded, and hopped back
into her sleeping quarters. Molly was sure
that the hutch was actually bigger on the
inside, as it seemed to have at least four
rooms. "I shall have a rest," Snowdrop said
grandly. "This has been rather a tiring
day." She lay down on her back in the

hay, with her paws in the air, and closed her eyes. "You could bring me some grated carrot later, perhaps," she suggested. "As a little bedtime something..."

After tea, Dad came back out with Molly to check that Snowdrop was settling down well in her new home. Molly grinned to herself when Dad said this. Sometimes she wished she could tell him that some of the animals spoke to her. But she didn't think he would believe her – he would say she'd imagined it. Right now it would be fun to be able to say that Snowdrop was fine – but she'd asked for grated carrot for supper, and she didn't approve of the view from her hutch, because the lawnmower was too grubby. Molly had promised to wipe it.

"I wonder if that medicine's working

yet?" Dad said thoughtfully to Molly as they walked down the garden. "Have you noticed Snowdrop hiccupping at all today?"

"No." Molly shook her head. "Maybe she's better. It would be great to be able to tell Albert we'd cured her, wouldn't it?" Molly skipped ahead excitedly as Dad stopped to see how his flowerbeds were looking. She would love to be able to welcome Albert back on Tuesday with the news that Snowdrop was all better.

But just as she opened the shed door – it was sticking a bit, so it took a minute – Molly heard a hiccup. Not very loud, but definitely a *hic!* She sighed. Oh dear... There was another one, and another, and then a flash of golden light lit up the hutch. Molly caught one glimpse of Snowdrop's startled face, peeping out of the wire front of the hutch, and then there was a loud *pop!* and she disappeared.

Then Dad walked into the shed – to find Snowdrop gone.

Molly was peering into the back of the hutch, trying to work out if Snowdrop was still there, just invisible, or if she'd actually *gone* somewhere.

"Molly, what are you doing?" Dad

asked, sounding surprised. "Snowdrop's not going to like you sticking your head in her hutch like that! Can you get her out for me, so I can check her over?"

Molly closed her eyes tightly, then opened them again and looked back in the hutch, hoping that Snowdrop would have miraculously reappeared. But she hadn't.

"No."

Dad blinked. "What?"

"I can't get her out . . . she, umm . . . she isn't here, Dad. . ." Molly twisted her fingers worriedly. What else could she say?

"But — but where is she? Molly! You can't have lost her, we've only had her for a day? What happened?" Dad sounded really cross. "Did you leave the hutch open?"

"No! Of course not!" Molly said, her

voice hurt. She was far too sensible to do
that!

"Molly, you must have done, how else
could she have got out? I knew this was
a bad idea." Dad shook his head. "Right,
you search in here, see if she's hiding
behind any of the gardening things, and
I'll go and look outside. I just hope she
hasn't got out of the garden, we might
never find her." Dad rushed out on to

the lawn, and Molly followed him, trying to explain, but what could she say? Dad wasn't going to believe that Snowdrop had vanished all by herself.

Molly walked back into the shed, and stared anxiously into Snowdrop's hutch. "Snowdrop! Snowdrop!" she whispered. "Please come back! I'm really worried about you, and Dad's so cross, he thinks I let you out. Please come back as soon as you can!"

Nothing happened. Molly could hear Dad calling crossly in the garden and running up and down, searching under the bushes.

"Please, Snowdrop!" she whispered again.

All at once there was another flash of golden light, and Snowdrop was back. She was sitting on top of her hutch now, looking slightly dazed. "*Hic!*" she said loudly. And then, "Hello, Molly!"

"Sssshhh! My dad's here, he's looking
for you. He thinks you're lost. Please will
you get back in your hutch, he's so cross!"

Snowdrop sighed, and let Molly slip
her back into the hutch, just as Dad came
striding back into the shed. "There's no sign,
Molly. This is why Mum and I were worried
about you having a pet. You have to be so
careful – hey, where did she come from?"

"She was there all the time, Dad!" Molly said, trying to smile, and shutting the hutch door *very* tightly. "I think she was hidden behind her hay bed, I just couldn't see her!" She felt a bit guilty, because it wasn't strictly true. But after all, she hadn't left the door open, and Snowdrop hadn't *really* gone out of the shed, had she?

"But I looked too. . ." Dad muttered.

"She just wasn't there. You are one tricksy bunny," he told Snowdrop sternly. "I'm getting a bad feeling about this weekend." He sighed. "Don't be long, Molly, all right? And make sure you close that hutch up tightly! I don't trust that rabbit, at all..."

Chapter Four

Snowdrop at School

Molly tried to get Snowdrop to explain where she'd been, so she'd be able to find her if it happened again, but Snowdrop said she didn't know.

"It was somewhere sparkly," she said, not very helpfully. "And it smelled nice."

It wasn't a lot to go on.

Molly just had to hope that Snowdrop wouldn't get hiccups when Dad was around. She didn't think he'd believe the story about losing Snowdrop in the hay *again*.

"I wish I knew how to cure you,"
she told Snowdrop on Sunday afternoon.
They were sitting in the shed doorway,
Snowdrop on Molly's lap, her eyes
blissfully closed as Molly stroked her ears
over and over.

"Mmm."

Molly got the feeling Snowdrop wasn't
really listening.

"Mum tells me to hold my breath and

count to ten when I get hiccups, have you tried that?"

"Rabbits aren't good at holding their breath," Snowdrop said, stretching her front paws out lazily, so that she was flopped all across Molly's lap.

"When I got hiccups at Grandad's house once, he gave me a spoonful of sugar to stop them, but I don't think sugar's good for rabbits..." Molly sighed.

Snowdrop's ears twitched with interest. "Perhaps we should try..." she said hopefully.

Molly giggled. "Snowdrop, you are so greedy!"

"I only want to cure my hiccups," Snowdrop protested, trying to look innocent.

Molly tickled her ears. "I'll miss you when I'm at school tomorrow," she said sadly.

Snowdrop sat up at once. "School? You mean you won't be here?"

"Well, no, tomorrow's Monday! I have to go to school, Snowdrop, even though you're here. I'm really sorry. You don't get days off because of rabbits."

"Well, you should..." Snowdrop muttered grumpily. "I don't like being on my own, it's very boring. I wanted to go to the conference, and I wasn't allowed, and now you're leaving me too!"

Snowdrop sulked on and off for the rest of the day, until Molly brought her a whole bowl of grated carrot before she went to bed. Then she let Molly kiss her nose, and even said sorry for being so bad-tempered.

But the next morning Snowdrop had had an idea. "Can't I come to school too?" she asked hopefully.

"No!" Molly said, sounding horrified.
"We aren't allowed pets at school, ever!
I mean, we do have a school guinea pig,
but we can't bring our own pets into
school. I'm sorry, Snowdrop. I just came
to fill up your food and water bowls.
And I brought you some beautiful carrots,
see. . ."

Snowdrop sniffed. But then her eyes
brightened, and she picked up one of
the carrots in her teeth. As Molly took
out the bowls to refill them, Snowdrop
hopped up on top of the hutch, where
Molly had left her lunch box. Snowdrop
wasn't just any rabbit after all. She had
learned lots of useful tricks with Albert,
and she was quite capable of opening
a lunch box, without even using magic.
She quickly dropped the carrot inside,
and glanced back down at Molly, who

was still making sure there were lots of
sunflower seeds in her food bowl.

"Albert said you really liked them, so
I'm giving you some extra ones, OK?"

Snowdrop blew a waft of glittery,
golden breath on the carrot that made it
go all sparkly. She twitched her nose in

a satisfied sort of way, and nudged the
lunch box shut. Done. "That's hardly any!"
Snowdrop protested, peering down at her

food bowl. "Lots more than that!"

Molly shook a few more in. "There you go! You've got loads now. Have a nice day, and I'll be back by afternoon snack time! See you later!"

"Goodbye, Molly!" Snowdrop watched her carefully shutting the hutch door. She was planning to see Molly a little sooner than Molly thought...

Rabbits seemed to keep popping up at school that morning. The maths problems were about how long it would take how many rabbits to eat a field of lettuces, and two of Molly's friends had new rabbit pencil cases. It made Molly jittery. She really hoped Snowdrop was behaving herself!

At lunch time, Molly sat and stared at her lunch box. She didn't really feel hungry. But she could feel one of the teachers watching her, so she opened it up at last.

There was a carrot inside.

A whole carrot, with the green feathery leaves still on the top. Molly blinked at it. Mum sometimes gave her carrot sticks in a little pot, but not a whole one! It looked awfully like one of the carrots she'd given Snowdrop that morning...

As she stared, the carrot started to

sparkle – just little golden glimmers round the leaves. Molly gulped, and grabbed it, hiding it in her lap. Luckily all her

friends were complaining about the test
Miss Fraser had given them that morning
(which Molly couldn't even remember)
and hadn't noticed. Molly quickly took
off her cardigan, and put it over the
carrot. She had a horrible feeling she
knew what was about to happen.

She was right. There was a funny little
noise, rather like a hiccup, and a flash of
golden light, which luckily was mostly
hidden under Molly's cardigan. Then the
cardigan wriggled, and Snowdrop's silvery-
white nose peeped out.

"Hello Molly!" she squeaked excitedly.
"I've come to school too!"

"How did you get here?" Molly
whispered, tucking Snowdrop's ears back
under her cardigan. "We mustn't let
anyone see you!"

"I put a finding spell on the carrot,

so I could follow it when I hiccupped.
It was very clever of me. Aren't you
impressed?" Snowdrop sounded smug.

"Of course I am, but we're going to get
into trouble. I told you, we aren't allowed
pets!" Molly looked round anxiously, but
no one seemed to have spotted that she
was talking to her cardigan.

Snowdrop wasn't listening. "I'm soooo
hungry! It was hard work, that spell," she
moaned.

"Eat the carrot!" Molly said crossly.

"I'm bored with carrots now. I'd like something else. Maybe some lettuce. Have you got any?" Snowdrop started to creep out from under the cardigan, and Molly grabbed her in horror.

"No!"

"OW!" Snowdrop squeaked loudly, and everyone looked at Molly. Molly looked behind her, trying to pretend she didn't know what the noise was either. Then there was another *pop!* and a flash, and Snowdrop wasn't huddled under Molly's cardigan any more.

So where was she?

Knowing Snowdrop, Molly thought, she would be looking for food. She'd wanted lettuce. Molly looked round to see if anyone had lettuce in their sandwiches. She had to get Snowdrop back before

someone spotted her... Then she noticed
a spot of white over by the dinner
queue – Snowdrop had found the salad
bar! She was sitting happily on the edge
of a big metal tray of lettuce, nibbling
away blissfully.

Molly stood up, wondering how on
earth she was going to get Snowdrop

out of there without anyone seeing her. But she was too late. There was a sudden scream, and one of the dinner ladies threw a ladle at Snowdrop. "It's a rat!" she yelled, then she fainted with horror, collapsing in a heap behind the counter.

Snowdrop jumped into the air in panic, then there was an enormous *pop!* and she disappeared completely, leaving everyone wondering just what was going on.

Molly ran across the room, hunting for Snowdrop, but she couldn't see her anywhere. It didn't help that half the girls in the school (and some of the boys) thought Snowdrop had been a rat too, and were standing on their chairs screaming.

Molly spent the whole of lunch time searching, but Snowdrop was nowhere to be seen. She'd got such a fright,

Molly just didn't know where she might have gone. She was really hoping that Snowdrop had jumped back to her hutch, where she would feel safe. But when Molly finally got back from school, and raced down the garden to the shed, there was no welcoming squeak from Snowdrop's hutch. It was quite empty.

Molly sat down on the step, blinking away tears. Crying wouldn't help. Snowdrop was gone – and Molly had no idea how to get her back.

Chapter Five

The Sparkly Spell

Molly sat staring out into the garden, desperately trying to think of places Snowdrop might be. She couldn't give up! She just hoped that Snowdrop wasn't frightened, or hurt.

There was a rustling in the bushes, and Molly looked up sharply. It was only a blackbird, but Molly got up to search round the garden anyway. Snowdrop didn't seem to have an awful lot of control when she disappeared without expecting to. Maybe she'd aimed for her hutch and missed?

She was just peering under the wheelbarrow that Dad had left out, when Kitty came up behind her, very quietly. "What are you doing?" she asked, and Molly jumped and banged her head on the wheelbarrow.

"Nothing!" she snapped crossly. But it was lucky that it had been Kitty who caught her, not Mum or Dad. She mustn't let them find out that Snowdrop had disappeared! She had to find her first!

But as Molly realized this, Dad came walking down the garden. "Mum wants you, Kitty. Hi Molly, how was school? Have you been to see Snowdrop? Did she miss you today?"

"Mmm!" Molly didn't know quite what to say. She cast an anxious glance down to the shed, at the bottom of the garden.

"I'll just have a quick look at her before tea." Dad carried on down the path.

"Oh, no, she's all right!" Molly gasped out.

"It's OK, Molly, I'm sure she's fine – you've done so well looking after her." Dad put an arm round Molly's shoulders. "I have to say, Molly, I'm really impressed.

You've been very responsible."

Molly felt sick — she'd been hoping that Dad would say something like this, and she'd been waiting for her parents to notice how well she was looking after Snowdrop, but why did it have to be *now*? When Dad was just about to find out that Snowdrop was gone. Molly suddenly knew that she couldn't — mustn't — let Dad see the empty hutch.

But what was she going to do? Suddenly the magical locket that Sparkle the kitten had given her seemed to grow warm around her neck under her school shirt. Molly put her hand up to it. It felt glittery and buzzy and special, and Molly took a deep breath. It was like a magical message from Sparkle, telling her she had to do a spell — but Molly had never done magic on her own before.

Dad had let go of her and was strolling on, muttering to himself about needing to cut the grass, it was full of daisies. He was right.

The daisies made Molly think of Snowdrop, and her fussy daisy-eating. Her eyes pricked with tears. Molly knelt down and picked a handful of daisies, hurriedly pulling off the petals one by one.

Dad was almost at the shed now.

Molly closed her eyes and threw the handful of daisy petals up in the air, whispering, *Stop him!* to herself. They seemed to hang in the late afternoon light for a few seconds, fluttering and shimmering silver. Then they floated down, and some of them landed in Molly's dad's hair. He stopped, and ran one hand across his face, looking confused.

"Oh, Molly, now what was I meant to be doing? It's always the same, you get down to the end of the garden and forget what you went for." He sighed, and wandered slowly back to the house.

Molly stared after him, with her mouth hanging open. That was the first time she had done magic all by herself – and it had worked! A thrill of delight ran through her – she felt so proud!

But there was no time to celebrate, she still had a missing bunny to find...

Worn out from searching all afternoon, Molly cried herself to sleep that night. She couldn't help imagining Snowdrop, lost and alone somewhere, probably frightened, with no idea how to get home. Albert was coming home tomorrow, and he would be really looking forward to seeing her. How could Molly tell him Snowdrop was lost?

But in the middle of the night, Molly woke up with a jump. She'd been dreaming of carrots. Feathery-leaved, orange and green and silver-sparkly carrots. Just like the one that Snowdrop had used in her naughty spell to appear at school. Molly sat up in bed, staring into the darkness, her breathing fast and trembly with excitement. The carrot – she still had the carrot! It was in her school bag, wasn't it?

Molly slid out of bed, tiptoed across her floor, and made for the stairs as fast as she could. She crept down them in the darkness, feeling her way by hugging the banister. There was a little moonlight shining through the glass in the front door, so she could almost see. Her school bag was sitting in the hallway, and Molly ferreted through it. There was something round, and cold – no, that was a water bottle... But here it was! She could feel the cool, feathery leaves, and the tingle of magic as her fingers closed round it. Molly dashed back up the stairs, and curled up back in her bed, holding the carrot in shivery hands.

"Snowdrop! Snowdrop!" she whispered. "Where are you? Find your way back!"

There was a flash of golden, glittering light, like there had been at school, and Molly caught her breath excitedly, sure that Snowdrop would come bouncing on to her bed.

But she didn't. No bunny hiccupped, and the carrot was just a carrot again.

Chapter Six

A Cure For Hiccups

Molly woke to hear Mum calling her from the doorway.

"Molly! Molly! Wake up! You haven't overslept, have you? You must have had a busy day at school yesterday. Get dressed and come down quickly, Molly, Albert's here! He drove all night to get back and see Snowdrop, he was missing her so much."

Molly blinked sleepily. Albert. Snowdrop. It took a few seconds for the names to mean anything, then it all flooded back.

Albert was here to fetch Snowdrop, and Molly didn't have her!

The spell hadn't worked, and Molly had fallen asleep again eventually, still clutching the carrot. She felt awful. She could hear Albert's voice downstairs, talking to Mum and Dad. He sounded happy and excited, as though he'd had a great time at the conference. There was an eager tone to his voice as well. Obviously he was waiting for Molly to come down and take him to see Snowdrop. It was nice of him to wait.

Molly sniffed, burying her nose in her pillow. She didn't want to get up and tell everyone the truth. Oh, why hadn't it worked? The carrot was on the pillow next to her, the long green leaves tickling her chin.

And giggling. Molly opened her eyes, slowly. She was fairly sure that even

carrots with spells on them didn't giggle.
But magical rabbits did, and their whiskers
were tickly and tingly...

"Oh, do wake up!" a soft little voice
muttered in her ear. "Come on, Molly,
haven't you missed me?"

It *had* worked! Molly sat straight
upright, almost knocking Snowdrop off
her pillow. "Where *were* you?" she gasped.

Snowdrop shuddered. "I don't know! It was horrible, it was *very* far away, and it was all dark. I didn't like it at all. I was so happy when I heard you calling me. It took a while to get back, that was all. I'd been trying to look for Albert, but it was hard when I'd never been to that Edinburgh place."

"Ohhh!" Molly breathed, hugging Snowdrop delightedly. "I thought it hadn't worked! I was so worried about you!"

Snowdrop nudged Molly's chin with her nose, in a sorry sort of way. "I shouldn't have followed you to school, Molly, it was my own fault I got lost in that dark place, and you saved me. Albert will be very grateful."

Molly jumped out of bed. "Did you hear? Mum said he's downstairs. I need to get dressed and get down there."

"And you need to get me back into my hutch!" Snowdrop pointed out. "Albert wouldn't mind me being up here, but I don't think your mum would like it. Can I take the carrot? I'm starving!"

Molly was pulling on her school uniform. "Can't you magic yourself back?" she asked, halfway inside her shirt.

Snowdrop was silent for a minute. Then, "I don't think so," she said doubtfully. "I think something's happened... I'm sure I can disappear with you or Albert to help me, but I don't think I can do it on my own any more. The hiccup feeling's gone, and that's what was making me jumpy..."

"You're not hiccupping any more? Really?" Molly picked Snowdrop up and stared at her thoughtfully. "But that's amazing! You're cured! I wonder how, though?"

Snowdrop gave a little shiver. "Well, I don't *know*, but I think that horrible woman throwing something at me had something to do with it. Every time I want to hiccup, I can't help thinking of her! Uugggh!"

Molly laughed. "Of course, a fright! That's the best cure for hiccups there is! It's what Dad always tries to do when me or Kitty have them, only he's useless at it and he just makes us laugh. I can't believe we solved the problem without even trying!"

Snowdrop nodded. "It's a pity, I shall miss those funny magic jumps. But Albert will be relieved. Please, Molly, I do want to see him so much. If you hold me, and we both think of my hutch, I'm sure I can get there. Then you can go down and fetch him for me."

"OK." Molly held Snowdrop tightly, and thought of the pretty, blue-painted hutch, the sweet-smelling hay bed, Snowdrop's food bowls...

There was a twinkling fizz of golden light, and Snowdrop disappeared from her arms. Molly looked at the suddenly empty space, and giggled. She'd just done another spell! But now she had to get downstairs to see Albert! She flung open her bedroom door, and raced to the stairs.

"She looks wonderful!" Albert said admiringly, stroking Snowdrop's tummy as she lay on her back in his arms.

Molly looked round to check that Mum and Dad weren't listening. "And we cured the hiccups!" she whispered. "Snowdrop will tell you – she got a bit of a fright, and now she can't hiccup-jump any more!"

"Oh, Snowdrop, were you doing something you shouldn't? I told you to be good for Molly," Albert sighed.

"I was only a little naughty," Snowdrop yawned. "Molly is very nice, but I did miss you. You know how to peel carrots exactly right." She rubbed her ears against his sleeve lovingly.

Molly grinned at Albert. She had loved having Snowdrop as a borrowed pet, but she *was* bossy!

"Molly did well, don't you think, Albert?" Molly's dad asked, as he came out of the shed, lugging Snowdrop's hutch.

"Oh, very well. Better than you can imagine!" Albert said, smiling.

"Like I said before, Molly, I'm really proud of you." Dad glanced at Mum, and she nodded. "You know, we think you're almost ready for a pet of your own."

Molly beamed at them both, and then caught Snowdrop's eye. The silver-white rabbit's fur twinkled pink for just a second, and she winked.

Molly winked back. She was so

happy – she'd wished for a pet when Star
and Stella gave her a wish, and now it
was starting to come true. And she'd done
magic, all by herself! That was almost
as exciting. Perhaps she'd be able to use
her spells to help another magical animal
soon...

Read more about Molly's magical adventures!

She can talk to animals!

Molly's Magic

The Witch's Kitten

HOLLY WEBB

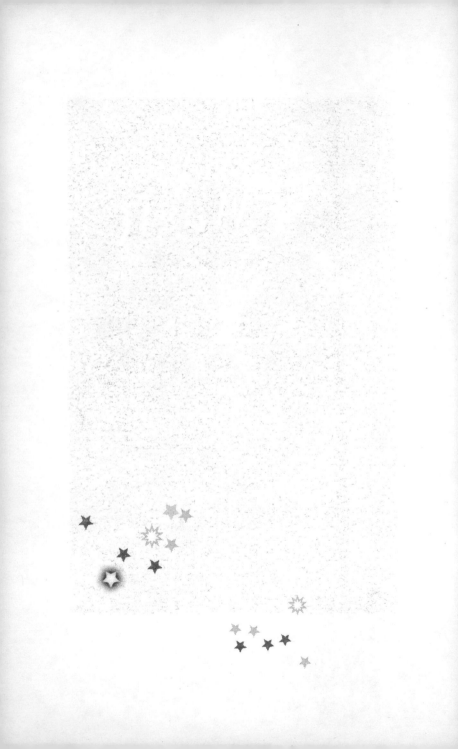

She can talk to animals!

Molly's Magic

The Wish Puppy

HOLLY WEBB

She can talk to animals!

MOLLY'S Magic

The Secret Pony

HOLLY WEBB

If you liked this book, try these!

And coming soon. . .

HOLLY WEBB is the author of the bestselling *Lost in the Snow* and its sequel, *Lost in the Storm*, as well as the popular Triplets series. She has always loved cats and now owns two very spoilt ones.